DILEMMAS IN
DEMOCRACY

Corruption in Politics

Kate Shoup

 Cavendish
Square

New York

Published in 2020 by Cavendish Square Publishing, LLC
243 5th Avenue, Suite 136, New York, NY 10016

Library of Congress Cataloging-in-Publication Data

Names: Shoup, Kate, 1972- author.
Title: Corruption in politics / Kate Shoup.
Description: New York : Cavendish Square, [2020] | Series: Dilemmas in
democracy | Audience: Grades 7-12. | Includes bibliographical references and index.
Identifiers: LCCN 2018056897 (print) | LCCN 2019000318 (ebook) | ISBN
9781502645029 (ebook) | ISBN 9781502645012 (library bound) | ISBN 9781502645005 (pbk.)
Subjects: LCSH: Political corruption--Juvenile literature. |
Political ethics--Juvenile literature.
Classification: LCC JF1081 (ebook) | LCC JF1081 .S455 2020 (print) | DDC 364.1/323--dc23
LC record available at https://lccn.loc.gov/2018056897

Editorial Director: David McNamara
Editor: Caitlyn Miller
Copy Editor: Alex Tessman
Associate Art Director: Alan Sliwinski
Designer: Christina Shults
Production Coordinator: Karol Szymczuk
Photo Research: J8 Media

The photographs in this book are used by permission and through the courtesy of:
Cover Tetra Images/Getty Images; background (and used throughout the book) Artist Elizaveta/
Shutterstock.com; p. 4 Leemage/Corbis via Getty Images; p. 8-9 PeopleImages/iStock/Getty Images;
p. 13 Owen Franken/Corbis/Getty Images; p. 16 Joana Toro/VIEWPress/Corbis/Getty Images; p. 18
Jeff Malet Photography/Newscom; p. 20-21 Pressmaster/Shutterstock.com; p. 24, 28 Corbis/Getty
Images; p. 31 David J. & Janice L. Frent/Corbis/Getty Images; p. 32 Graphica Artis/Getty Images; p.
34 AP Images; p. 40-41 Thomas Ives/The LIFE Images Collection/Getty Images; p. 44 Mark Wilson/
Getty Images; p. 46 Narinder Nanu/AFP/Getty Images; p. 49 Frederic Legrand Comeo/Shutterstock.
com; p. 50 Florian Gaertner/Photothek/Getty Images; p. 54 360b/Shutterstock.com; p. 57 Xinhua/
Alamy Stock Photo; p. 58 Oliver Contreras/SIPA USA/AP Images; p. 60-61 Mark Reinstein/
Shutterstock.com; p. 64 GRECO/Wikimedia Commons/File:GRECO logo.svg/PD; p. 67 UNODC/
Wikimedia Commons/File:UNCAC 1.png/PD; p. 68 STR/AFP/Getty Images; p. 71 ScreenShot.

Printed in the United States of America

CONTENTS

CHAPTER 1

What Is Corruption?

Corruption is when a public official, such as an elected politician or appointed government official, uses his or her political power for personal gain or to maintain power. Or, as political scientist Joseph Nye says, corruption is "the abuse of public office for personal enrichment."

Scholars have considered the problem of corruption since ancient times. Even the ancient philosopher Aristotle weighed in on the matter. To him, governments that showed "a regard to the common interest" and were built according to "strict principles of justice" were "true forms" of government. In contrast, governments that "regard only the interest of the rulers" were "defective" and "perverted." In other words, they were corrupt.

Aristotle felt that the rulers of "true" (noncorrupt) forms of government focused on the common good, and only on the common good. This means they never put their own interests above those of their community. More modern thinkers say this might not be a reasonable expectation, as it does not

Opposite: The Greek philosopher Aristotle was among the first to consider the problem of corruption.

consider human nature—which is not always virtuous. Taking human nature into account, perhaps a looser definition of political corruption is required: the use of one's public office for personal enrichment that violates certain limits. (Of course, what those limits might be is a matter of debate!)

Often, people confuse corruption with ethics (or lack thereof). According to the Merriam-Webster dictionary, ethics is "the discipline dealing with what is good and bad and with moral duty and obligation." Corruption and ethics are related, however. When a government acts in an unethical manner, corruption may be the result.

The same goes for scandal. A scandal is an action or event that flies in the face of morality or decency. Although all incidents of corruption are (or should be) considered scandals, not all scandals involve corruption. For example, suppose a public official were caught cheating on his or her spouse. This behavior might rightly be seen as scandalous, but it is not corrupt.

Corruption is much more common in countries ruled by dictators than in democracies. This is because dictators are free to act in secret and outside the bounds of law and have no fear of losing power through the electoral process (either because there is no such process or because the process itself is corrupt). Still, corruption does occur in democracies—even in liberal democracies, which value free elections, openness, and rule of law.

Not all corruption occurs in politics or government, though. Corruption can also exist in businesses, religious organizations, and even sports organizations. In these other spheres, it is not usually a public official who engages in the corruption. Instead, it might be the CEO of a company, a minister or priest, or an official whose job is to govern a particular sport. This book, however, focuses on corruption in politics and governance.

Classifying Corruption

There are three main classes, or levels, of corruption: grand corruption, political corruption, and petty corruption. Grand corruption describes the abuse of high-level power—for example, the presidency—to enrich a few people at the expense of everyone else. More often, it involves stealing huge sums of money—millions or even billions of dollars—from the country's treasury.

Political corruption is less obvious. It involves manipulating political policies, institutions, and procedural rules to hold onto power, status, or wealth. For example, someone who commits political corruption might introduce a law that benefits him or her personally.

Finally, petty corruption is when a lower-level public official demands a "toll" of some sort from everyday citizens seeking basic services—like at a hospital, school, police department, passport office, or other agency.

Types of Corruption

Corruption comes in many forms, each with its own unique characteristics. In most cases, officials engage in corruption to benefit themselves financially. Sometimes, however, people perform corrupt actions in exchange for information.

Perhaps the most common type of corruption is bribery. Bribery is when someone gives money, goods, or services (in other words, a bribe) to a public official in exchange for some type of favor.

Some forms of corruption involve bribing public officials with cash or other valuables.

This might be a lucrative government contract or job, access to people in power, or even a promise that the public official will vote a certain way on upcoming legislation. Suppose the owner of a paving company paid local officials to grant him a hefty contract to repave a major road. That would be bribery. (This is often called a *quid pro quo*—Latin for "something for something.")

Although some bribes are initiated by the "giver," others start with the "taker." For instance, a public official might require a citizen to pay to obtain or speed up some government service or to land some type of government job. That payment is, of course, on top of whatever the citizen already pays in taxes to support the official's salary! This type of bribery is called extortion.

Bribery is extremely common—particularly in less-developed countries. According to the International Monetary Fund, public officials (and others) around the world accept $1.5 trillion in bribes each year.

Another form of corruption is influence peddling. This is when a powerful person or organization makes a large financial contribution to an elected official's reelection campaign rather than paying the official directly. In exchange, the donor expects the official to act in his or her interest. They might expect the official to vote a certain way on upcoming legislation or to eliminate some type of burdensome regulation. Typically, the donor is represented by a third party called a lobbyist.

When it comes to campaign funds, there are strict rules. Misuse of these funds—like diverting them for personal use—is yet another form of corruption. So, too, is obtaining campaign donations from illegal sources, such as federal government contractors or foreign nationals.

Then there are kickbacks. Also similar to a bribe, a kickback is a payment made to a public official who delivers a contract, job, or other benefit to the payee. Unlike a bribe, a kickback is paid after the fact. Recall the paving-company example from earlier. If the owner of that company were to pay the official who granted him a contract to repave a major road some portion of the money earned from that contract, that would be a kickback.

Like kickbacks, a form of corruption called embezzlement—also known as graft—also involves the transfer of money. This time, however, the money flows from the government into the hands of a public official. If a public official in charge of an expensive project were to move a portion of that project's budget into his or her own account, that would be embezzling.

One form of embezzling is the misuse of public funds or resources. This is when a public official spends public money unwisely (as when a public official spent more than $30,000 in public funds on a dining set for his office) or uses public resources to handle their own personal business (like the official who recently directed employees to help his nephew with a high school project).

Rather than stealing money from the government, some embezzlers divert it from foreign aid. Foreign aid is money donated by outsiders, usually to help care for the country's poor. This form of corruption—common in developing countries—is particularly cruel as it prevents the country's most vulnerable people from getting much-needed help. According to experts, there is plenty of money to improve the lives of poor people in developing countries and perhaps even end world hunger completely. This variety of corruption (along with a general lack of organization in developing countries), however, prevents this from happening.

What Are Lobbyists?

A lobbyist is someone who works on behalf of a client. Lobbyists "lobby" to influence elected public officials to make laws or rules that benefit that client. In exchange, the lobbyist's client typically donates to the public official's reelection campaign. This client might be a large corporation, such as a drug company; an organization that advocates for some type of issue, such as gun safety or climate change; or an association that represents an industry, such as coal or health care.

Lobbyists can be an important partner in the lawmaking process. Often, they help officials grasp the pros and cons of a particular law or policy. However, some people think lobbyists have too much influence on the outcome of this process. They say elected officials are much more likely to listen to a person or organization that contributed to their reelection campaign than to one that didn't—especially if that person or organization contributed a lot. Opponents of lobbying also accuse elected officials of acting more in the interests of lobbyists and their clients than in those of their actual constituents or for the greater public good.

Lobbyists frequently visit lawmakers on Capitol Hill on behalf of their clients.

Some public officials even join with criminal elements for their own personal gain. For example, an official might shield members of a drug-smuggling ring from law enforcement in exchange for some portion of its profits.

Regardless of how corrupt officials obtain money—through bribery, kickbacks, embezzlement, etc.—they often engage in money laundering to conceal its source. Money laundering is when someone makes money that comes from one (illegal) source seem like it came from another (legitimate) source. People do this by depositing "dirty" money into one or more legitimate banks. They then make several transactions with the money to make it hard to trace. This might mean transferring it to different accounts in other names, placing it in one or more untraceable bank accounts overseas, investing it in a shell company (which is a fake company that exists solely to launder money) or even a legitimate business, running it through a casino, or buying luxury items like a yacht or mansion. Eventually, they simply retrieve the money and keep it for themselves.

Some types of corruption involve giving preferential treatment rather than stealing money. Preferential treatment is when a public official offers jobs or contracts to someone—even if that person lacks the qualifications to carry it out. There are three types of preferential treatment. One is nepotism. This is when the job or contract goes to a family member. Another is cronyism, which is when the official gives the job or contract to a personal friend. Finally, there's patronage. This is when the official hands a job or contract to a political supporter or campaign donor. A variation of preferential treatment is pay to play. This is when a public official puts a contract or job up for the highest bidder.

While some forms of corruption enrich the public official (or his or her family and friends) personally, others allow the official to maintain his or her hold on their power. An example of this type of corruption is election fraud. This involves interfering with the process or outcome of an election. Someone might commit election fraud by registering voters illegally, preventing people who are legally entitled to vote from registering, limiting voters' access to polls, intimidating voters at the polls, hacking into voting machines, hindering the counting process, or deliberately miscounting votes. Using government forces to suppress political opposition is another type of corruption, as is the practice of police brutality against certain groups.

The Effects of Corruption

The effects of corruption are widespread. Transparency International (TI), a global organization that fights corruption of all kinds, divides these effects into four main categories: political, economic, social, and environmental.

On the political front, corruption undermines democracy. Abraham Lincoln described democracy as "government of the people, by the people, for the people." Corruption turns this vision of government on its head. Corrupt public officials—even if elected "by the people"—aren't "of the people," and they certainly don't govern "for the people." They seek only their own enrichment.

When this happens, a negative cycle begins. When a person sees corrupt public officials act only in their own interests rather than in his or her interest or more generally for the public good, they become cynical and mistrustful of their government. When people become cynical and mistrustful of their government, they stop

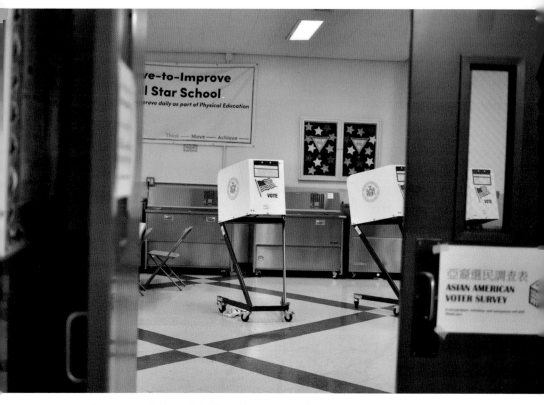

When people lose faith in a democracy due to corruption, they often stop voting.

participating in the political process. When people stop participating in the political process, it gives corrupt public officials even more power, enabling them to enrich themselves even more.

The end result of all this is that the so-called democratic government loses its legitimacy. (A government that does not have legitimacy is one that is seen as not conforming to laws or rules.) Indeed, as hopes for reform fade, the government might stop being a democracy altogether. This outcome is particularly dangerous, threatening both stability and peace. Stability and peace might also be threatened by enraged citizens who may join with extremist groups to fight the government. "Every country that harbors an extremist insurgency today suffers from kleptocratic governance," writes journalist Sarah Chayes. Sometimes, these insurgent groups even manage to overthrow the corrupt government.

Equally damaging is the effect of corruption on the economy. The economy in a corrupt country simply cannot work properly. This explains why, according to the World Bank, the average income in countries with high levels of corruption is just one-third of that in countries with a low level of graft.

There are many reasons for this. One is that corruption drives investors away. Another is that resources are distributed inefficiently and unfairly. Third, as greedy officials steal from the country's treasury, it drains the country of its wealth. That's not all. Corruption also raises the price of goods and services—which are often of lower quality (if they are available at all). These higher prices have a greater impact on poor people, who are less able to absorb the cost. The result is increased income inequality—yet another economic effect of corruption.

One might argue that the social effects of corruption are in part a result of the economic effects. In other words, as greedy public officials steal money from the country's coffers that *should* be spent on social services—things like education, health care, housing, infrastructure, and sanitation—everyday people lack access to much-needed government services.

In extremely corrupt societies, these same everyday people also find themselves victim to other forms of corruption, such as bribes, kickbacks, and preferential treatment. Scholar Ankie Hoogvelt describes this scenario:

Kleptocracies

Kleptocracies are nations subject to extreme corruption.

A nation subject to extreme corruption of all types is called a kleptocracy. This is a Greek word that means "rule by thieves." In a kleptocracy, a small group of "elites" controls all levers of power. They use this power to pass laws that benefit themselves, install judges who will rule on cases in their favor, plunder the country's treasury, exploit the country's natural resources for their own gain, and assume command of the military for their own use. Bribes and preferential treatment are particularly common in kleptocracies.

Kleptocracies are a type of oligarchy. An oligarchy is a government run by a small group of people, such as a single family or the members of a certain religion. It's rare for an oligarchy to exist in a democracy, but it can happen if the citizens of that democracy become uninformed and disengage from the political process. Similar to an oligarchy is a plutocracy. This is when the leaders of the oligarchy are all quite wealthy. Oligarchies and plutocracies discourage the practice of democracy.

Patients [offer] bribes to nurses in hospital to persuade them to pass on a bed-pan; traffic offenders [bribe] police officers to waive the fine; tax collectors [add their own fee]; ... educational officers [give] government scholarships to their cousins; and political candidates [buy] the votes of entire electoral districts.

All this adds up. Indeed, families in Mexico spend as much as 14 percent of their income on bribes just to obtain basic goods and services, like water, medicine, and education. For the poorer members of society, this takes a significant toll.

As for the effects of corruption on the environment, consider that corrupt political officials frequently strip their country of natural resources for their own personal gain and ignore regulations (if they even exist) meant to protect the environment—all to increase their own profits. The result is often the destruction of entire ecological systems, not to mention rampant pollution, toxic water, and poisoned soil.

These environmental effects aren't limited to the country in question. Because they contribute to climate change, they affect us all—melting ice caps, which causes rising seas; triggering droughts, which affects the global food supply; producing extreme weather, such as record-breaking temperatures and devastating storms, which causes property damage and even loss of life; and more.

Key Contributors to Corruption

There are many contributors to corruption. One major contributor is a lack of transparency in government. In other words, corrupt public officials are free to act as they wish because they know their actions will be hidden. This explains why countries that support freedom

Corruption happens in the shadows.

of the press to report on the actions of public officials, that pass laws to ensure its citizens have access to information about government activities, and whose populations are highly literate experience less corruption. On a related note, countries that fail to measure corruption and report the results are also at risk of increasing it.

Another contributor is weak rule of law. For example, there might be laws to prevent public officials from engaging in corrupt activities, but if these laws are not enforced—by police or by courts of law—then the corruption is likely to continue and perhaps even grow.

Corruption also becomes more likely when power is held by a small group of people who are related in some way. This group might consist of members of the same family, clan, or tribe; people who share the same religion; people of the same ethnicity; and people of the same social class. Furthermore, corruption increases if society breaks down—such as in the cases of war or natural disaster.

Finally, corruption might increase in countries with large public sectors. A country with a large public sector is one in which the government provides lots of services (rather than relying on private businesses to do so). This is especially true if a country has complicated regulations and lacks transparency. Note, however, that some countries with large public sectors are notoriously not corrupt. Nordic countries—Denmark, Finland, Norway, Sweden, and Iceland—have very large public sectors. Yet, the 2017 Transparency International Corruption Perceptions Index ranked them as the second, third, fourth, sixth, and thirteenth *least* corrupt countries in the world, respectively. And officials in some corrupt countries use privatization—that is, the transfer of responsibility for state services into private hands—as a way to enrich friends and family.

Scholars view corruption as a byproduct of a society's values. To members of affected societies, behaviors that others would describe as "corrupt" are perfectly acceptable. Unless these societies change their values, the corruption will likely continue. Experts suggest this might be achieved through improvements to the country's economic and political institutions.

Transparency International

Founded in 1993, Transparency International (TI) has one vision: "a world in which government, business, civil society, and the daily lives of people are free of corruption." To realize this vision, TI, headquartered in Germany, has established more than one hundred chapters worldwide to fight corruption, offer free legal advice, assist whistleblowers who challenge corrupt public officials, and more.

TI believes that the first step to eliminating corruption is to expose it. To achieve this, the organization conducts a yearly assessment to rank the level of corruption in 180 countries and territories worldwide. This involves surveying hundreds of thousands of people around the globe. The organization then publishes the results of the assessment in a report called the "Corruption Perception Index." A poor score on the index, the organization states, "raises questions that can't be ignored ... For leaders, the pressure is on to answer." In 2017, this list flagged Somalia as the world's most corrupt country. New Zealand was the least corrupt.

The Corruption Perception Index measures perceptions of corruption rather than actual corruption. This is because corruption, which generally happens in secret, is hard to detect, let alone measure. Still, TI argues that "perceptions matter in their own right, since ... firms and individuals take actions based on perceptions."

In addition to corruption in the political arena, TI also exposes corruption in business. To reduce this type of corruption, TI has established benchmarks to measure corporate integrity and transparency and set global standards for corporate behavior. Finally, TI highlights the effects of corruption on other key issues, including poverty and climate change, and partners with organizations that specialize in these areas to help them tackle these problems.

THE "BRAINS"

CHAPTER 2

Corruption in the United States

By the late 1700s, American colonists had assembled a long list of complaints about their British rulers. At the top of this list was corruption. They saw British tax collectors as dishonest and believed they simply used the money they collected to line their own pockets. Indeed, this perceived corruption was one of the main reasons for the American Revolution.

Tammany Hall

Corruption in America did not end with the defeat of the British, however. One example of corruption in early American politics relates to an organization called Tammany Hall. Founded in New York City in 1789, Tammany Hall originally provided services for members of the middle class, but later changed course to cater to immigrants—particularly from Ireland. Eventually, Tammany Hall became *the* machine

Opposite: Political cartoons like this one by artist Thomas Nast helped bring down Boss Tweed of Tammany Hall.

behind the Democratic Party in New York and even expanded nationwide before its collapse in the mid-1960s.

At first Tammany Hall was a legitimate organization (for the most part). That changed in 1858 when a scrappy New York City politician named William "Boss" Tweed took over control of the organization. Assisted by a group of like-minded associates, Tweed used various forms of corruption—from bribery, to voter fraud, and beyond—to position some twelve thousand Tammany men in key city jobs. These recruits sent lucrative city contracts to companies controlled by the group, called the Tweed Ring. The companies then overbilled for work done (as well as work *not* done). On one construction project alone, the Tweed Ring pocketed $8 million ($157,481,220 today)—all for a building that was never even completed. All told, the Tweed Ring stole anywhere between $40 million and $200 million (equivalent to $787,406,100 and $3,937,030,501 today).

In the summer of 1871, the *New York Times* published a series of articles that revealed the extent of the Tweed Ring's corruption. These articles, along with a series of political cartoons by artist Thomas Nast that showed Tweed as enormously bloated to convey his gluttony and greed, turned public opinion against him.

Police arrested Tweed in December 1871, and he was convicted of a host of corruption charges in 1873. Due to various legal technicalities, however, Tweed spent the next few years in and out of prison, before escaping to Spain via Cuba in spectacular fashion. When a Spanish officer recognized Tweed from one of Nast's cartoons, he was promptly returned to America. Tweed died in prison while awaiting trial in 1878.

The Crédit Mobilier Scandal

Another case of corruption, called the Crédit Mobilier scandal, occurred around the same time as Boss Tweed's corruption. In 1862, the US Congress passed the Pacific Railroad Act. It provided for the construction of a new railroad line, called the Transcontinental Railroad, that would stretch 1,750 miles (2,820 kilometers) from the Missouri River to the California coast. The government hired two companies, the Central Pacific Rail Road (CPRR) and the Union Pacific Rail road (UPRR), to construct the line. These companies would assume operation of the line after its completion.

Railroad executives knew they could make more money building the line than operating it after it was complete. This was because the railroad passed primarily through unpopulated terrain—meaning few customers would be interested in traveling there, at least in the short term. To make sure they turned a quick profit, officials and stockholders at the UPRR came up with a sneaky scheme. They formed a new company called Crédit Mobilier of America but did not reveal that they were the owners of this new firm. They then directed the UPRR to hire Crédit Mobilier to handle the construction of the UPRR's portion of the railroad.

This by itself was unethical. But what was worse was that Crédit Mobilier purposely charged the UPRR inflated prices for work done on the line—charges that the UPRR passed on to the US government, along with fees of its own. That meant when the company distributed profits to company officials and stockholders, they were paid twice. One of those payments—the one from Crédit Mobilier—was far larger than it should have been!

Pictured here are the directors of the UPRR in 1866.

The scheme didn't stop there. In 1867, company officials became concerned that the US government might stop paying the inflated prices to complete construction on the railroad. In response, they offered cash bribes and deeply discounted stock shares in Crédit Mobilier to several members of Congress and other powerful politicians. This was to ensure Congress would continue to pay for the project and keep the plot going.

In 1872, a New York newspaper called the *Sun* found out about the Crédit Mobilier scheme and quickly reported on the story. Soon after, the US House of Representatives launched an investigation into the matter. In 1873, the House formally censured two members of Congress who had accepted bribes from Crédit Mobilier and UPRR officials. (A censure is a formal expression of disapproval.)

The Whiskey Ring and Teapot Dome Scandals

Two years after the Crédit Mobilier scandal, another scandal involving public officials in cahoots with private businesses broke: the Whiskey Ring scandal. This scheme was simple. Instead of paying the US government 70 cents tax per gallon of whiskey sold (as required by federal law), whiskey makers paid public officials 35 cents per gallon. These public officials then marked the tax as having been paid. In this way, whiskey makers saved 35 cents per gallon sold, and public officials diverted millions of dollars of tax revenue into their own pockets.

When US Secretary of the Treasury Benjamin Bristow caught wind of the scheme, he organized a series of raids nationwide. These yielded more than 200 indictments—including one of

President Ulysses S. Grant's personal secretary, Orville Babcock. In the end, Babcock wasn't convicted, but 110 others were.

Then there was the Teapot Dome scandal. In 1922, Secretary of the Interior Albert Bacon Hall secretly leased an oil field under the control of the US Department of Interior called Teapot Dome to Harry F. Sinclair of the Sinclair Oil Company. Hall also leased two other oil fields under government control, called Elk Hills and Buena Vista, to Edward L. Doheny of Pan American Petroleum and Transport Company.

In both cases, Hall leased the oil fields without opening them up to other bidders. As a result, the terms of both leases were quite favorable to Sinclair and Doheny. As it happened, this was entirely legal. What was *not* legal was that Doheny had issued Hall a no-interest loan of $100,000 ($1,490,326 today) in exchange for the lease—essentially a bribe. Hall also received more than $200,000 ($2,980,652 today) in war bonds from a company owned in part by Sinclair.

Later that year, an oilman from Wyoming learned about these secret leases. In response, he wrote an angry letter to Senator John B. Kendrick. Two days later, Kendrick called for an investigation into the deals. The investigation bore little fruit—until detectives discovered evidence of the $100,000 loan from Doheny to Hall.

In 1929, Hall was convicted of accepting the bribe from Doheny and sent to prison—the first member of a president's cabinet to face time behind bars. Strangely, however, Doheny was not convicted of *giving* the bribe to Hall. Adding insult to injury—at least from Hall's point of view—a company owned by Doheny foreclosed on

The Teapot Dome scandal rocked American politics. Here, politicians refer to the scandal in campaign materials for the 1924 presidential election.

Hall's home due to "unpaid loans." (Sinclair also escaped conviction for bribery but did face six months of jail time for jury-tampering, or attempting to influence the jury in his case.)

The Emoluments Clause

The Founding Fathers included a special clause in the US Constitution to prevent political leaders from profiting from their positions.

The US Constitution includes a section called the "Title of Nobility" clause, often referred to as the "Emoluments Clause." (An emolument is a payment or profit gained from holding public office.) This clause reads as follows:

> *No Title of Nobility shall be granted by the United States: And no Person holding any Office of Profit or Trust under them, shall, without the Consent of the Congress, accept of any present, Emolument, Office, or Title, of any kind whatever, from any King, Prince, or foreign State.*

The Founding Fathers included this clause in the Constitution to prevent government officials from profiting from their position, and to ensure their loyalties remained with the United States.

Critics of President Donald J. Trump claim he is in violation of this clause. They say this is because the Trump Organization, which is a company owned by President Trump, conducts business with foreign governments and receives payments from them. As of 2019, this matter was under review by US courts.

Reporters Carl Bernstein (*left*) and Bob Woodward (*right*) of the *Washington Post* broke the Watergate story.

Watergate

For decades, the Teapot Dome scandal was *the* most notorious example of corruption in American politics. Indeed, the phrase "Teapot Dome" became synonymous with corruption. That changed in the early 1970s after a series of events called the Watergate scandal.

On May 28, 1972, five "burglars" broke into the office of the Democratic National Committee (DNC) in the Watergate office complex in Washington, DC. Their primary mission was to plant recording devices inside the office to spy on the DNC. At first, it seemed as if this mission had gone without a hitch. Within a matter of days, however, the devices stopped working. So, on June 17, the men broke into the office a second time to fix them. This time, they were caught.

Investigators quickly guessed that the break-in and recording devices were connected in some way to an organization called the Committee to Re-Elect the President (CRP). CRP had formed in 1971 to support the reelection campaign of Republican president Richard M. Nixon in the upcoming 1972 presidential election. Investigators' first clue was that one of the burglars, James W. McCord Jr., was the security coordinator for CRP and a former Nixon aide. Their second clue was that two of the burglars had contact information for a top Nixon White House official in their address books. As it happened, the investigators were right. CRP was involved in the break-in. Indeed, CRP had conceived and bankrolled the operation in an attempt to gain an edge over the Democratic candidate in the upcoming election.

CRP officials, members of Nixon's staff, and even Nixon himself scrambled to cover up CRP's role in the burglary. CRP and White House officials and staff burned transcripts of conversations recorded by wiretaps planted in the first break-in, planted false alibis for CRP operatives, and told investigators that the burglars were zealous anti-Communists who had acted alone. For his part, Nixon instructed an aide to order the FBI to halt its investigation of the break-in.

Despite Nixon's orders, the FBI stayed on the case. At the same time, reporters conducted investigations of their own. Using information from an anonymous source inside the FBI, two journalists named Bob Woodward and Carl Bernstein of the *Washington Post* reported that CRP officials weren't the only ones involved in the break-in and cover-up. Officials in the highest levels of the Justice Department, FBI, CIA, and White House were also involved. The journalists also revealed that the burglars had been paid by CRP. Finally, they reported that the Watergate incident "stemmed from a massive campaign of political spying and sabotage conducted on behalf of President Nixon's reelection and directed by officials at the White House." The attempted theft of information directed by government officials was a clear case of corruption.

As more and more details emerged through the press, the White House viciously attacked the reporters on the case to try to discredit them. Their efforts paid off. Most Americans believed these reporters were engaged in nothing more than a witch hunt. Indeed, Nixon won reelection that November in a landslide. Nixon's reelection was not the end of the Watergate affair, however. Both the FBI and members of the press continued their investigations.

In January 1973, all five Watergate burglars, along with a CRP official who had coordinated the break-in, either pleaded guilty or were convicted for their role in the break-in. Sensing that the burglars had withheld information about the break-in in court, the judge assigned to their cases urged them to speak out. Finally, one of the burglars admitted that top White House officials had pressured the men to lie about certain details of the break-in to protect the president and his top aides.

Some frightened White House officials began cooperating with the FBI. Others resigned. Still others were fired. Then, in May 1973, a bipartisan US Senate committee conducted a series of hearings on the matter. The hearings, which lasted for months, revealed that the Watergate break-in was just one of a series of secret operations carried out to weaken Democratic politicians—many funded through illegal or corrupt means. More importantly, they uncovered that Nixon had installed a recording device in the Oval Office to secretly tape all his conversations and phone calls.

Both the senators and Special Prosecutor Archibald Cox, who had been appointed by the Justice Department to separately investigate the scandal, knew these tapes were important to uncovering the truth. They issued subpoenas for the tapes. (A subpoena is a command to submit some form of evidence for a case under review by a court or other governmental body.) Nixon rejected the subpoenas, claiming "executive privilege" and "national security." Cox and the Senate refused to let up. For months, they hounded Nixon to release the tapes.

Nixon offered various compromises, including releasing written summaries of the tapes instead of the tapes themselves. These ideas were rejected. Irate, Nixon instructed Attorney General Elliot Richardson to fire Archibald Cox on October 20, 1973. Richardson declined. Nixon then ordered Deputy Attorney General William Ruckelshaus to do the deed. He too refused. After firing both men, Nixon turned to Solicitor General Robert Bork. Bork reluctantly complied. This chain of events became known as the "Saturday Night Massacre."

Pressure on Nixon let up—but only temporarily. A unanimous Supreme Court ruling issued in July 1974 forced him to release all relevant tapes to investigators. As had been predicted, one of these tapes revealed that Nixon had indeed ordered the FBI to halt the investigation into the Watergate break-in—a clear abuse of power. The tapes did not, however, conclusively prove that Nixon had anything to do with planning the break-in itself. (Some say the tapes *would* have proven this—had more than eighteen minutes of one tape not been "accidentally" erased.)

Even before Nixon released the tapes, Congress had filed articles of impeachment (charges filed that can lead to a president's removal) and conducted hearings on the matter. Afterward, given what the tapes contained, his conviction was all but certain. To avoid this, Nixon resigned from office on August 9, 1974—the first (and so far only) president ever to do so.

After Nixon resigned, Congress dropped impeachment proceedings. His successor, President Gerald Ford, granted a full and unconditional pardon for any crimes Nixon "committed or may have committed or taken part in" while president. Others weren't so lucky. In all, sixty-nine people—including senior White House officials and cabinet members—were indicted. (To be indicted is to be formally accused or charged of a crime.) Of these, forty-eight either pleaded guilty or were convicted.

The Abscam Scandal and the Keating Five

Although Watergate remains the most notorious example of corruption in American politics to date, it was hardly the last. One example of post-Watergate corruption was the Abscam scandal. In 1978, FBI agents enlisted a con artist named Melvin Weinberg to pose as the US representative of a fake company owned by a fictitious Arab sheikh to draw in white-collar criminals. Over time, Weinberg and various FBI agents shifted their focus from white-collar crime to political corruption. They conducted stings to lure in crooked politicians by offering cash in exchange for political favors. In all, the team snared five Democratic congressmen and one Republican. All six were convicted of bribery and conspiracy in 1981. Despite Abscam's success, however, many viewed the operation in a negative light, accusing the agents involved of entrapment, or tricking people into committing a crime.

Another scandal was called the Keating Five. In the early 1980s, Congress eliminated regulations in the banking industry to allow banks to make riskier investments. Soon, however, federal regulators became worried that these investments were *too* risky. They exposed the federal government, which pays back certain types of customer funds if a bank collapses, to significant financial losses. Regulators instituted new rules to limit these risky investments. They also began investigating certain banks, including one called the Lincoln Savings and Loan Association, which was run by a man named Charles Keating.

In 1987, Keating bribed five US senators with large campaign donations to interfere with the investigation. These senators—four Democrats and one Republican—became known as the Keating Five. When news of these donations broke in 1989, the Senate Ethics Committee reviewed the matter. After a lengthy investigation, despite clear evidence of bribery, Senate officials formally reprimanded one of the Keating Five—not for breaking any laws, but for violating Senate norms. The other four senators were deemed merely to have "used poor judgment" or "acted improperly." These are not the only cases of corruption to rock American politics in the post-Watergate era, but they are two of the more famous ones.

Political Corruption Today

American politicians continue to engage in corruption, even today. Indeed, as of the time of this writing, two members of the Trump administration had been forced from their jobs due to allegations of corruption.

Charles Keating ran
the Lincoln Savings and
Loan Association. He
bribed five US senators
to interfere in a federal
investigation of the bank.

In September 2017, Secretary of Health and Human Services Tom Price was forced to step down after spending nearly $1 million in taxpayer money to charter private planes and military jets for travel instead of booking cheaper seats on commercial flights. Price's behavior was seen as "particularly shocking," wrote one Democratic senator, because he had served "in an administration that routinely calls for draconian spending cuts and a reduction in government waste," and had himself "repeatedly advocated for fiscal restraint."

Then, in July 2018, Scott Pruitt, the head of the Environmental Protection Agency, resigned under pressure. This was in response to more than a dozen investigations into allegations ranging from corruption for personal gain; to using government staff for personal projects; to lavish spending of public funds on travel, offices upgrades (including the construction of a soundproof booth at a cost of $43,000), security, and more. One fellow Republican, a congressman, described Pruitt's conduct as "grossly disrespectful to American taxpayers."

Corruption has also occurred in recent years at the state level. One case involved Democratic governor Rod Blagojevich from Illinois. When Illinois senator Barack Obama won the presidency in 2008, it was Blagojevich's job to appoint a new senator to replace him. Rather than selecting the best person for the job, Blagojevich took bribes from people who wanted the position. This was just one example of influence peddling by Blagojevich. He also committed extortion and fraud and lied to federal agents. The Illinois General Assembly impeached and convicted Blagojevich in January 2009, removing him from office. Blagojevich was also convicted in federal court of various crimes. In December 2011, Blagojevich was sentenced to fourteen years in prison.

Transparency International's US Corruption Barometer

In addition to its Corruption Perceptions Index, Transparency International releases an annual US Corruption Barometer, which measures the perception of corruption inside the United States.

According to the 2017 barometer, 44 percent of Americans believed the current president and his White House staff were corrupt, up 8 percent from the prior year. Members of the legislative branch didn't fare much better: 38 percent of Americans believed that most or all members of Congress engage in corruption. And 70 percent of Americans said US government institutions aren't doing enough to fix these problems, perhaps indicating a lack of faith in the American form of government.

One might argue that these Americans overestimate the level of corruption in American politics. After all, in Transparency International's 2017 Corruption Perceptions Index, the US rates a respectable sixteenth—tied with Austria and Belgium, and just ahead of Ireland and Japan. Nevertheless, there's always room for improvement!

Scott Pruitt, head of the Environmental Protection Agency, resigned in July 2018 after allegations of corruption. Here, Pruitt speaks at a conference in June 2018.

Another governor, Republican Bob McDonnell of Virginia, and his wife, Maureen, also faced federal corruption charges. Their crime: accepting more than $135,000 in gifts, trips, and loans from a political donor. The pair were convicted of several charges in September 2014 and sentenced to two years in prison. However, the US Supreme Court vacated the conviction in 2016. That is, they said the conviction was void and cleared the McDonnells of the charges.

The McDonnell case created a legal precedent for corruption cases. Legal precedents are cases that judges look to when making their decisions. Supreme Court justices decided that the McDonnells were not guilty of corruption because their actions were "distasteful," but they did not qualify as "official [government] acts." The Supreme Court decision said that the McDonnells had not broken corruption laws and that courts needed to be careful about what can be considered corruption. All nine Supreme Court justices were unanimous in this decision.

Going forward, judges and lawyers will compare cases to the McDonnell case. It is likely to set a standard for what is corruption and what is not. The case raises a larger point, though: corruption is not always as clear-cut as it seems. There is a gray area between actions that are frowned upon and actions that break the law. This is one reason that corruption can be difficult to tackle in modern America.

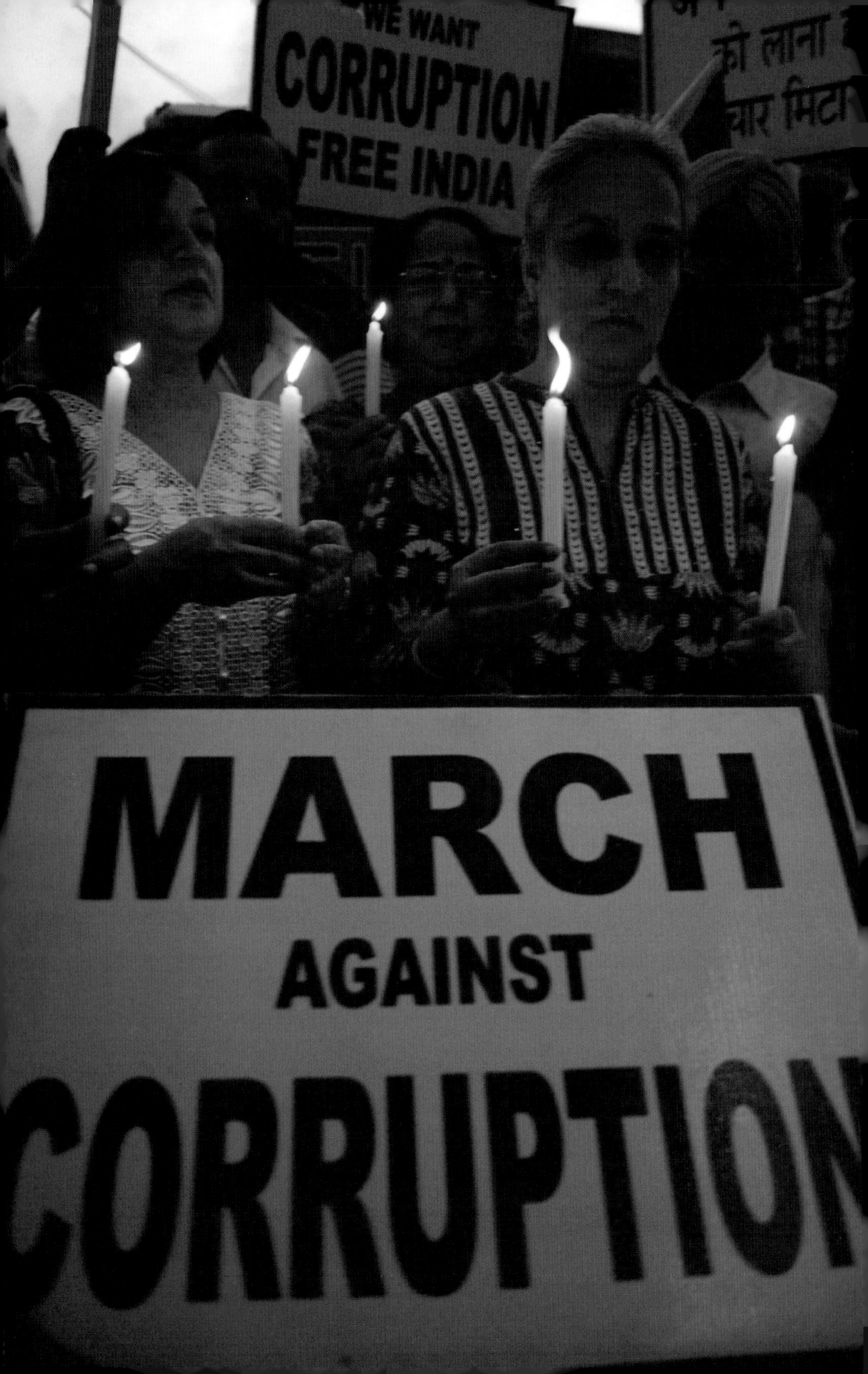
WE WANT
CORRUPTION
FREE INDIA
MARCH
AGAINST
CORRUPTION

CHAPTER 3

Corruption Around the World

The degree of corruption in the United States can feel concerning. Yet in truth, the United States—which ranked 16 (out of 180) in the Transparency International 2017 Corruption Perceptions Index—is relatively clean compared to many other countries. Corruption is far more common in other countries—even in some liberal democracies.

Corruption in India

One example of a liberal democracy that suffers from corruption is the Republic of India. Indeed, corruption has plagued India since it gained its independence from Great Britain in 1947. Much corruption in India is of the petty variety—that is, corruption by lower-level public officials who demand bribes from everyday citizens or small businesses to get things done. This behavior is especially common among officials in charge of distributing licenses and permits required

Opposite: Activists in India protest corruption at a 2011 march.

to conduct business. Officials in this role simply refuse to issue licenses unless they are paid a bribe first. However, these officials are not the only ones who demand bribes. Customs officials, tax collectors, and other officials also do so. This helps explain why, according to a recent survey, more than half of people who live in India have paid a bribe to access public services or institutions. The monetary value of all this petty corruption amounts to nearly $5.5 billion each year.

Recently, however, grand corruption has become more common in India. An example of this is the Bofors scandal, which occurred during the 1980s and 1990s. In this scandal, several Indian politicians, including the country's prime minister, received almost $9 million (more than $17 million today) in kickbacks from a Swedish weapons maker called Bofors in exchange for purchasing weapons for the Indian military.

Another example of grand corruption in India was the 2G spectrum scam, which occurred starting in 2008. In this case, public officials from one political party accepted bribes from mobile phone companies who wanted licenses to use the 2G phone network. They then granted the licenses to these companies for much less than they were worth—indeed, an estimated $39 billion less. That was money that should have gone to the Indian government to provide services for Indian citizens. This scandal caused huge protests in the nation's capital city of Delhi. It also prompted politicians from other parties to shut down Parliament for three weeks in protest. In 2012, the Supreme Court of India ruled that the officials had "virtually gifted away important national asset[s]" and canceled the licenses. However, in 2017, a special court in Delhi declared the officials involved in the scheme innocent of any crimes.

Indian prime minister Narendra Modi ran on an anti-corruption platform but has had only limited success fixing the problem.

Vladimir Putin

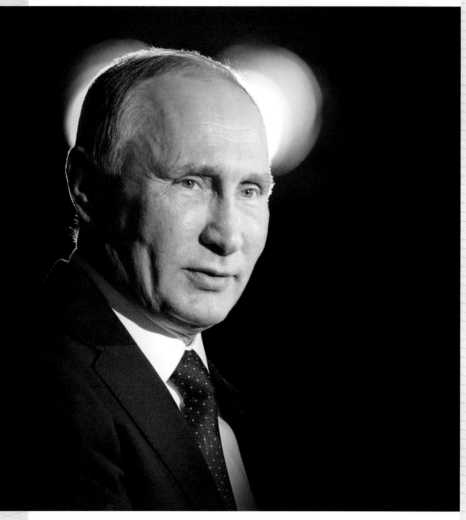

Russian president Vladimir Putin is believed to be one of the most corrupt politicians in the world.

Longtime Russian president Vladimir Putin is widely viewed as among the most corrupt public officials on Earth. A former KGB spy, Putin not only controls the Russian government and its secret police, he also heads up several large state-owned companies, giving him near total power over the country's economy.

Experts estimate that through sheer corruption, Putin has amassed a personal fortune of upwards of $200 billion, making him one of the richest men in the world. Some say Putin maintains his hold on his wealth and power by eliminating his critics—such as journalist Anna Politkovskaya, mysteriously murdered in 2006, and political opponent Boris Nemtsov, shot dead in 2015.

It appears that Putin has recently hit on a new way to expand his power: by dismantling democracy abroad—even in the United States. According to former US Director of National Intelligence James Clapper, "Russian President Vladimir Putin ordered an influence campaign in 2016 aimed at the US presidential election" to "undermine public faith in the US democratic process." Putin also sought to undermine Democratic presidential candidate Hillary Clinton's "electability and potential presidency" because of a "clear preference for President-elect Trump." (Whether President Trump was aware of Russia's apparent involvement was under review as of 2019.)

As early as 1962, the Indian government assembled a committee to address the problem of corruption. Members of the committee observed that "there is a widespread impression that failure of integrity is not uncommon among ministers and that some ministers … have enriched themselves illegitimately, obtained good jobs for their sons and relations through nepotism, and have reaped other advantages inconsistent with any notion of purity in public life." However, the corruption continued.

Recent years have seen renewed efforts to crack down on corruption. These were inspired in part by a seventy-four-year-old activist named Kisan Hazare, who went on a hunger strike in 2011 to protest government corruption. He succeeded in drawing incredible attention to the issue and even pushed Indian lawmakers to pass an anti-corruption bill. Then, in 2014, Indians elected a new prime minister named Narendra Modi, whose campaign focused on the problem of corruption. After his election, Modi took a dramatic step to address the issue: he made certain forms of currency illegal and replaced them with a fresh type of currency. He then gave Indian citizens forty days to exchange the old currency for the new type. This forced public officials (and others) who had obtained secret stashes of cash through bribes and other forms of corruption to declare it and pay taxes on those funds.

At first it seemed Modi's approach to fighting corruption might work. India rose from eighty-fifth in the 2014 Transparency International Corruption Perceptions Index to seventy-sixth two years later. But in 2017, it fell to eighty-first place—tied with Morocco and Turkey—suggesting that perhaps Modi's efforts haven't succeeded after all.

Hamid Karzai and Afghanistan

Another democracy that suffers from extreme corruption is Afghanistan. In fact, corruption in Afghanistan is so terrible, it ranks 177th out of 180 countries in the Transparency International 2017 Corruption Perceptions Index. This is no doubt in part because Afghanistan—a rough and remote country situated in Central Asia—has experienced tremendous instability for decades.

Afghanistan wasn't always unstable. Between 1926 and 1973, Afghanistan operated under a constitutional monarchy whose rulers sought to modernize it. By the 1960s, says the BBC, "a new constitution transformed Afghanistan into a modern democracy, with free elections, a parliament, civil rights, emancipation for women, and universal suffrage." However, a series of events starting in 1973 led to the takeover of Afghanistan by a violent Muslim militia group called the Taliban in 1996. This group enforced harsh totalitarian rule based on an extreme version of Islam. In 2001, the United States invaded Afghanistan in search of Osama bin Laden, who was the mastermind behind the attacks of September 11, 2001. Within a matter of weeks, US forces had removed the Taliban from power, and a new leader named Hamid Karzai was installed. (For his part, Osama bin Laden escaped capture until 2011.)

At first, Karzai ruled on a provisional basis, but in 2004, he was elected president. Corruption quickly took root. Indeed, by 2009, according to the US Agency for International Development, corruption in Afghanistan had become "pervasive, entrenched, systemic, and by all accounts now unprecedented in scale and reach." Bribery and extortion became so rampant, wrote journalist Declan Walsh in 2012, "that corruption [could] no longer be described as a cancer on the system: it [was] the system."

Hamid Karzai served as Afghanistan's first democratically elected head of state. Karzai's administration was plagued with corruption.

Perhaps the most notable case of corruption in Afghanistan was the Kabul Bank scandal. Between 2010 and 2013, close Karzai associates, including his brother, stole $980 million from Kabul Bank and dispersed the funds to themselves, their families, and their friends. But this is far from the only example of Afghan graft. After the US invasion in 2001, Afghan officials diverted billions of dollars of US aid into their own private accounts. Yet they weren't the only ones to blame. To stay in Karzai's good graces as the war dragged on, US officials delivered tens of millions of dollars of US taxpayer money to him—sometimes in suitcases, backpacks, and shopping bags—and did not follow up to see how it was spent.

After serving two terms as president, Karzai stepped down in 2014. The corruption that characterized Karzai's reign has continued under his replacement, though. Indeed, Afghans widely view corruption as more of a problem than the Taliban, which has regained strength and influence in recent years.

The World's Most Corrupt Country: Somalia

According to the 2017 Corruption Perceptions Index, published by Transparency International, Somalia is the most corrupt country in the world, scoring a dismal 9 points out of 100.

"When it comes to corruption, no nation can compare to Somalia," *Forbes* reported in 2011. "Pirates seize ships at will, the al-Shabaab movement [a local militant group] terrorizes much of the country, and the ineffective Transitional National Government specializes in looting foreign aid intended for starving refugees." Indeed, said UN monitor Matt Bryden, "The scale of the [government's] financial hemorrhaging is so immense that the term 'corruption' seems barely adequate."

In early 2017, members of the Somalian government elected a new president, Mohamed Abdullahi "Farmajo" Mohamed. According to an aid group called the Enough Project, Farmajo "has a reputation for promoting good governance and combatting corruption." But, the organization acknowledges, he has "inherited a very difficult situation." Whether Farmajo will be successful in his efforts to eliminate corruption in Somalia remains to be seen.

Mohamed Abdullahi Mohamed was elected president of Somalia in 2017. He has pledged to stop corruption in his country.

CHAPTER 4

Combatting Corruption

Corruption is notoriously difficult to combat. Its secretive nature makes it hard to even identify, let alone fight. Often it's so widespread it seems impossible to gain even a foothold against it. Still, it must be fought to uphold democracy.

There is no one single way to combat corruption. Rather, the fight involves a multipronged attack that includes (but is not limited to) good governance, oversight by watchdog groups and NGOs, and public engagement.

Good Governance

Perhaps the most powerful weapon against corruption is simple good governance. This includes legislating against corruption (and enforcing these laws), encouraging transparency, guaranteeing a free press, protecting whistleblowers who call out corruption, and more.

Opposite: A free press is key to combatting corruption. Pictured here is the White House Press Corps in 2018.

Good governance is an essential means of stopping corruption. Members of US Congress introduce and pass laws that tackle corruption.

Lawmakers in the United States have passed legislation at the local, state, and federal level to combat corruption in all walks of American life—including politics. These laws are enforced by the Department of Justice (DOJ) and the Federal Bureau of Investigation (FBI). Lately, however, some of these laws—particularly those that affect the political sphere—have been weakened. This is due to recent Supreme Court rulings (including in the McDonnell case) that narrow the definitions of acts like bribery and extortion. Now these terms apply only to public officials who perform some "official act" that involves a "formal exercise of governmental power," such as voting for legislation or signing an executive order, on a donor's behalf. In other words, it is now legal for a public official to accept lavish gifts in exchange for activities as long as the activities are "unofficial." This can prove quite lucrative for the "giver" and the "taker." Thanks to these rulings, writes attorney Peter J. Henning, "buying access to elected officials is, in most cases, not a crime."

One way to ensure public officials adhere to anti-corruption measures—weakened or not—is to encourage transparency. Encouraging transparency might mean requiring public officials to disclose their financial interests. It could also include ensuring the government budget process is public. (Of course, certain spending, such as national defense spending, might need to remain private for national security reasons.) Finally, it might involve passing laws to allow free access to information about the government and its activities. An example of one such law is the American Freedom of Information Act (FOIA). The FOIA allows for the full or partial release of all US government documents (with some exceptions). According to the US government, "the basic function of the Freedom of Information Act is to ensure informed citizens." This, the government says, is "vital to the functioning of a democratic society."

More often than not, it's journalists, rather than police or other investigators, who root out corruption in government. This was true with the Tweed Ring, the Crédit Mobilier scandal, Watergate, and others. Therefore, it's critical that governments guarantee a free press. There's a reason America's Founding Fathers listed freedom of the press—along with freedom of religion, freedom of speech, the right to assemble, and the right to seek government assistance in resolving grievances—at the top of the Bill of Rights!

Simply put, countries that support freedom of the press to track the actions of public officials (rather than flatter and cater to these officials, as is often the case in less free societies), and whose populations have a high rate of literacy, experience less corruption. To quote Thomas Jefferson, "Where the press is free, and every man is able to read, all is safe."

Finally, laws to protect whistleblowers can also help make a dent in corruption. Too often, people who become aware of corruption stay quiet. They fear for their safety or their jobs. Whistleblower protection laws can help persuade them to come forward.

All this doesn't just happen. Fighting corruption requires a sustained effort and the will to carry it through—especially as the fight drags on. As Larry Noble of the American Center for Responsive Politics observes, "There is no end game" to the fight against corruption. It's "all part of the care of feeding of democracy."

Watchdog Groups and NGOs

Several watchdog groups and nongovernmental organizations (NGOs) are involved in the fight against corruption worldwide. Some of these groups relate specifically to corruption. Others include corruption among the list of problems they seek to solve.

GRECO is a nongovernmental organization whose mission is to monitor corruption and assess anti-corruption policies.

An example of an anti-corruption watchdog group is the Group of States Against Corruption (GRECO). Established in 1999, GRECO, which consists of representatives of forty-eight European countries as well as from the United States, "exists to uphold and further pluralist democracy, human rights, and rule of law and has taken a lead in fighting corruption as it poses a threat to the very foundation of these core values." Its main mission is to monitor corruption and to assess anti-corruption policies in government. Another example of a watchdog group is Interpol, which also monitors corruption (among other things). Interpol also coordinates with law enforcement worldwide to combat the problem.

In addition to these watchdog groups are several anti-corruption NGOs. One of these is Transparency International, which has been discussed throughout this book. Another is Global Witness. Founded in 1993, Global Witness has identified a strong link between rich natural resources, conflict, and corruption. The organization—which has offices in London; Washington, DC; and Brussels—works to break this link by spotlighting corrupt behaviors and practices.

Represent Us is another anti-corruption NGO. It brings together American "conservatives, progressives, and everyone in between to pass powerful anti-corruption laws that stop political bribery, end secret money, and fix our broken elections." There's also Anti-Corruption International, "a global youth movement committed to the eradication of corruption."

These are just a few watchdog groups and anti-corruption NGOs. For a more thorough list, see http://www.anticorruptionday .org/actagainstcorruption/en/resources/index.html.

Getting Involved in the Fight Against Corruption

We don't have to wait for public officials or NGOs to take action against corruption. People—including young people—can work to root it out themselves.

One way to root out corruption is to support a free press. That means reading newspapers whose reporters investigate corruption—or, even better, purchasing a subscription. Another way is to support anti-corruption NGOs by helping to publicize their efforts or by making a donation. People can also engage in the fight against corruption by supporting political candidates who run on an anti-corruption platform, and by marking International Anti-Corruption Day (December 9) in some way.

The UN Convention Against Corruption

The United Nations has become a powerful voice against corruption. In 2003, it created a legally binding global anti-corruption convention, called the United Nations Convention Against Corruption (UNCAC). (A convention is an agreement between nations. It is similar to a treaty but less formal.)

The UNCAC requires all joiners, called signatories, of which there are currently 186, to implement certain anti-corruption measures. These relate to technical assistance and information exchange, asset recovery, international cooperation, law enforcement, and the criminalization of corruption. It also paves the way for legal action against corrupt officials. Indeed, it was the UNCAC that enabled Transparency International to sue Teodorin Nguema Obiang, the son of president Teodoro Obiang Nguema of Equatorial New Guinea, for the theft of some $225 million in public money. Afterward, officials seized millions of dollars in assets gained through corruption and indicted the president's son. According to the organization, this set "a historic precedent for recovering dirty money worldwide."

9-11 December 2003 **Mérida, México** 9-11 de diciembre de 2003

Convención de las Naciones Unidas contra la corrupción

United Nations Convention against Corruption

 UNITED NATIONS
Office on Drugs and Crime

 NACIONES UNIDAS
Oficina contra la Droga y el Delito

The United Nations Convention Against Corruption was formed in 2003.

Indian activist Kisan Hazare serves as a reminder that individuals can have a big impact in the fight against corruption.

When evidence of corruption becomes public, people who seek to stop corruption should raise their voices in protest. That might mean using social media to speak out against the corruption or even assembling in public to make their feelings known. Even a single person can make a difference in the fight against corruption—like Kisan Hazare in India.

Of course, people can fight corruption by reporting corruption when they see it and refusing to participate in corruption themselves! All these steps are critical in maintaining healthy democracies. Healthy democracies cannot exist where there's widespread corruption. It's up to everyone to educate themselves and speak up. The stakes are high. Luckily, everyday people can (and do) help to stop corruption.

Tracking the Fight Against Corruption

The key to fighting corruption is to stay informed. This is not always easy, however. This is because most corruption happens in secret.

Fortunately, many journalists around the world work to uncover corruption. They publish stories about corruption in newspapers and magazines. One way to find these stories is to use Google. Simply type the word "corruption" in the search box and click the News link to see recent news stories that include that word. You can even set up a Google Alert to notify you by email when a newspaper or magazine publishes a story about corruption. (Note that you must have a Google account to do this.)

You can also follow anti-corruption groups on social media to stay informed about corruption. Twitter is an especially good place to follow anti-corruption groups. Several of these groups maintain a regular presence on the site, frequently offering links to articles about corruption worldwide, tips for getting involved, and other useful resources. Here's a brief list of Twitter accounts for anti-corruption groups:

* **Transparency International:** @anticorruption
* **Global Witness:** @global_witness
* **Anti Corruption International:** @anticorruptintl
* **Represent Us:** @representus

Global Witness's Twitter feed is a good resource for staying informed about corruption.

GLOSSARY

bribery When someone gives money, goods, or services (a bribe) to a public official in exchange for some type of favor.

corruption When a public official, such as an elected politician or appointed government official, uses his or her political power for personal gain or to maintain power. There are three categories of corruption: grand corruption, political corruption, and petty corruption.

divert To cause something to change course or direction.

election fraud The interference with the process or outcome of an election. Examples of election fraud include registering voters illegally, preventing people who are legally entitled to vote from registering, limiting voters' access to polls, intimidating voters at the polls, hacking into voting machines, hindering the counting process, and deliberately miscounting votes.

embezzlement The transfer of money from a government account into the hands of a public official. Also known as graft.

emolument A payment or profit gained from holding public office.

extortion Similar to a bribe but initiated by the "taker" rather than the "giver."

impeachment A formal charge of misconduct made against a public official.

influence peddling When a powerful person or organization makes a large financial contribution to an elected official's reelection campaign rather than paying the official directly.

kickback A payment made after the fact to a public official who delivers a contract, job, or other benefit to the payee.

kleptocracy A nation subject to extreme corruption of all types. In a kleptocracy, a small group of "elites" controls all levers of power to serve their own interests. Kleptocracy is Greek for "rule by thieves."

money laundering When someone makes money that comes from one (illegal) source seem like it came from another (legitimate) source.

pardon To formally release someone from the legal consequences of a crime.

preferential treatment When a public official offers jobs or contracts to someone, even if that person lacks the qualifications to carry it out. There are three types of preferential treatment: nepotism, which is when the job or contract goes to a family member; cronyism, in which the job or contract goes to a personal friend; and patronage, which is when the job or contract goes to a political supporter or campaign donor. A variation of preferential treatment is pay to play.

undermine To damage or weaken something (such as democracy).

whistleblower Someone who reports a crime such as corruption.

FURTHER INFORMATION

Books

Doeden, Matt. *Whistle-Blowers: Exposing Crime and Corruption*. Minneapolis, MN: Twenty-First Century Books, 2015.

Grayson, Robert. *The FBI and Public Corruption*. Broomall, PA: Mason Crest Publishers, 2009.

Miller, Debra A. *Hot Topics: Political Corruption and the Abuse of Power*. Farmington Hills, MI: Lucent Books, 2018.

Websites

International Anti-Corruption Day

http://www.anticorruptionday.org

Learn about International Anti-Corruption Day, which is held each December 9.

Transparency International Corruption Perceptions Index 2017

https://www.transparency.org/news/feature/corruption_perceptions_index_2017

Find out which countries score well—or poorly—in this corruption index.

United Nations Convention Against Corruption

https://www.unodc.org/unodc/en/corruption/uncac.html

Read about the United Nations's efforts to fight corruption worldwide.

Videos

Fighting Corruption Explained

https://www.youtube.com/watch?v=k_05pqhroiI

Learn more about what constitutes corruption and how corruption affects everyday people around the world.

Forget Nixon—Here Are the Most Corrupt US Politicians in History

https://www.youtube.com/watch?v=5tUGXQcj7Jc

Business Insider profiles three infamous politicians.

BIBLIOGRAPHY

Bernstein, Carl, and Bob Woodward. "FBI Finds Nixon Aides Sabotaged Democrats." *Washington Post*, October 10, 1972. https://www.washingtonpost.com/wp-srv/national/longterm/watergate/articles/101072-1.htm.

Brookings Institute. "Event Summary: Political Corruption in the United States and Around the Globe." April 28, 2004. https://www.brookings.edu/opinions/event-summary-political-corruption-in-the-united-states-and-around-the-globe.

Chayes, Sarah. "Corruption: The Unrecognized Threat to International Security." Carnegie Endowment for International Peace, June 6, 2014. http://carnegieendowment.org/2014/06/06/corruption-unrecognized-threat-to-international-security-pub-55791.

Drutman, Lee. 2015. "What We Get Wrong About Lobbying and Corruption." *Washington Post*, April 16, 2015. https://www.washingtonpost.com/news/monkey-cage/wp/2015/04/16/what-we-get-wrong-about-lobbying-and-corruption/?utm_term=.43607a3030cd.

Forbes. "Most Corrupt Countries." Accessed on November 9, 2018. https://www.forbes.com/pictures/eedh45gffgj/most-corrupt-countries/#3acb3cc1b5c9.

Henning, Peter J. "It's Getting Harder to Prosecute Politicians for Corruption." February 16, 2018. https://theconversation.com/its-getting-harder-to-prosecute-politicians-for-corruption-91609.

Hoogvelt, A. M. M. *The Sociology of Developing Societies.* London, UK: Macmillan, 1976.

Mulgan, Richard. "2. Aristotle on Legality and Corruption." In *Corruption: Expanding the Focus*, edited by Manuhuia Barcham, Barry Hindess, and Peter Larmour, 25–36. Canberra: Australian National University Press, 2012.

Nash, Nathaniel C., and Philip Shenon. "A Man of Influence: Political Cash and Regulation - A Special Report: In Savings Debacle, Many Point Fingers Here." *New York Times*, November 9, 1989. https://www.nytimes.com/1989/11/09/business/man-influence-political-cash-regulation-special-report-savings-debacle-many.html.

Transparency International. "Corruption Perceptions Index 2017." Accessed on November 6, 2018. https://www.transparency.org/news/feature/corruption_perceptions_index_2017?gclid=CjwKCAiA5qTfBRAoEiwAwQy-6QDveUkc-SPU3xLpDu0UA91jNT1M-d_fsEjmzJC7in3uIcr8hfZQVxoCpiQQAvD_BwE.

———. "FAQs on Corruption." Accessed on November 6, 2018. https://www.transparency.org/whoweare/organisation/faqs_on_corruption.

Walsh, Declan. "At Afghan Border, Graft Is Part of the Bargain." *New York Times*, November 11, 2014. https://www.nytimes.com/2014/11/12/world/asia/in-afghanistan-customs-system-corruption-is-part-of-the-bargain.html.

INDEX

lobbyist, 10, 12, **13**

McDonnell, Bob, 45, 62
Modi, Narendra, **49**, 52
Mohamed, Mohamed
    Abdullahi, 56, **57**
money laundering, 14

nepotism, 14, 52
Nixon, Richard M., 35–38
nongovernmental
    organizations (NGOs), 59,
    63–65

oligarchy, 18

pardon, 38
patronage, 14
petty corruption, 7, 47–48
political corruption, 5–7,
    14–16, 18, 19, 22, 23,
    38–39, 65
precedent, 45, 66
preferential treatment, 14, 17,
    18
Price, Tom, 42
protest, **46**, 48, 52, 69
Pruitt, Scott, 42, **44**
Putin, Vladimir, **50**, 51

rule of law, 6, 21, 64

Saturday Night Massacre, 37
scandal, 6, 27, 29–30, 34,
    38–39, 48, 55, 63
social media, 69, 70
Somalia, 23, 56
Supreme Court, 37, 45, 48, 62

Tammany Hall, 25–26
Teapot Dome scandal, 29–31,
    31, 34
transparency, 19, 22, 23, 59, 62
Transparency International
    (TI), 15, 22, 23, 43, 47,
    52–53, 56, 64, 66, 70
Trump, Donald J., 33, 39, 51
Tweed, William "Boss," **24**,
    26–27

undermine, 15, 51
United Nations Convention
    Against Corruption
    (UNCAC), 66, **67**
US Corruption Barometer, 43

watchdog groups, 59, 63–65
Watergate, 34, 36–39, 63
Whiskey Ring scandal, 29
whistleblower, 23, 59, 63
Woodward, Bob, **34**, 36

ABOUT THE AUTHOR

Kate Shoup has written more than forty books and has edited hundreds more. When not working, Shoup loves to travel, watch IndyCar racing, ski, read, and ride her motorcycle. She lives in Indianapolis with her husband and their dog.